What's Ur Your Hood, Orson?

Written by
the Holy Cross School Kindergartners
Albany, New York

Illustrated by Terry Kovalcik

SCHOLASTIC INC.
NEW YORK TORONTO LONDON AUCKLAND SYDNEY

Library of Congress Cataloging-in-Publication Data

What's under your hood, Orson? / written by the Holy Cross School
        kindergartners, Albany, New York; illustrated by Terry Kovalcik;
        [written by Erin Barber ... et al.].
            p. cm. — (My first library)
Summary: Charlie and Harriet, two cars who are friends, are reluctant
at first to drive with Orson because he is bigger and brighter than they are,
but they discover that underneath his hood he is just like them.
        ISBN 0-590-49247-0
        1. Children's writings, American. [1. Automobiles—Fiction. 2. Identity—Fiction.
3. Children's writings.] I. Kovalcik, Terry, ill. II. Barber, Erin. III. Holy Cross School
(Albany, N.Y.) IV. Series.
PZ7.55556 1993
[E]—dc20 92-33327

                                                        CIP
                                                        AC

Copyright © 1993 by Scholastic Inc.
Illustrations copyright © 1993 Terry Kovalcik
Designed by Bill SMITH STUDIO, Inc.
All rights reserved. Published by Scholastic Inc.
My First Library is a registered trademark of Scholastic Inc.
12 11 10 9 8 7 6 5 4 3 2 1   3 4 5 6 7 8/9
Printed in the U.S.A.
First Scholastic Printing, 1993

Once upon a time, in a little garage, there lived Harriet, a bright yellow car, and Charlie, a shiny blue car.

They drove together all the time.
They liked each other.

One day they drove to the park
to watch the children play.

While they were sitting there,
a new car came by. It was red.
It stopped.

The red car said,

Charlie and Harriet did not answer.
They were afraid. The red car was
too big, too shiny, and too bright.

They raced to their garage
and shut the door.

The red car started to follow, but soon stopped and began to cry.

Charlie and Harriet left the garage
and drove up to the crying car.
"What's wrong, Red?" asked Harriet.

"My name is not RED! It's Orson.
I ran out of gasoline and I want
to drive with you."

"You need gasoline too?" said Harriet.
"You want to drive with us?"

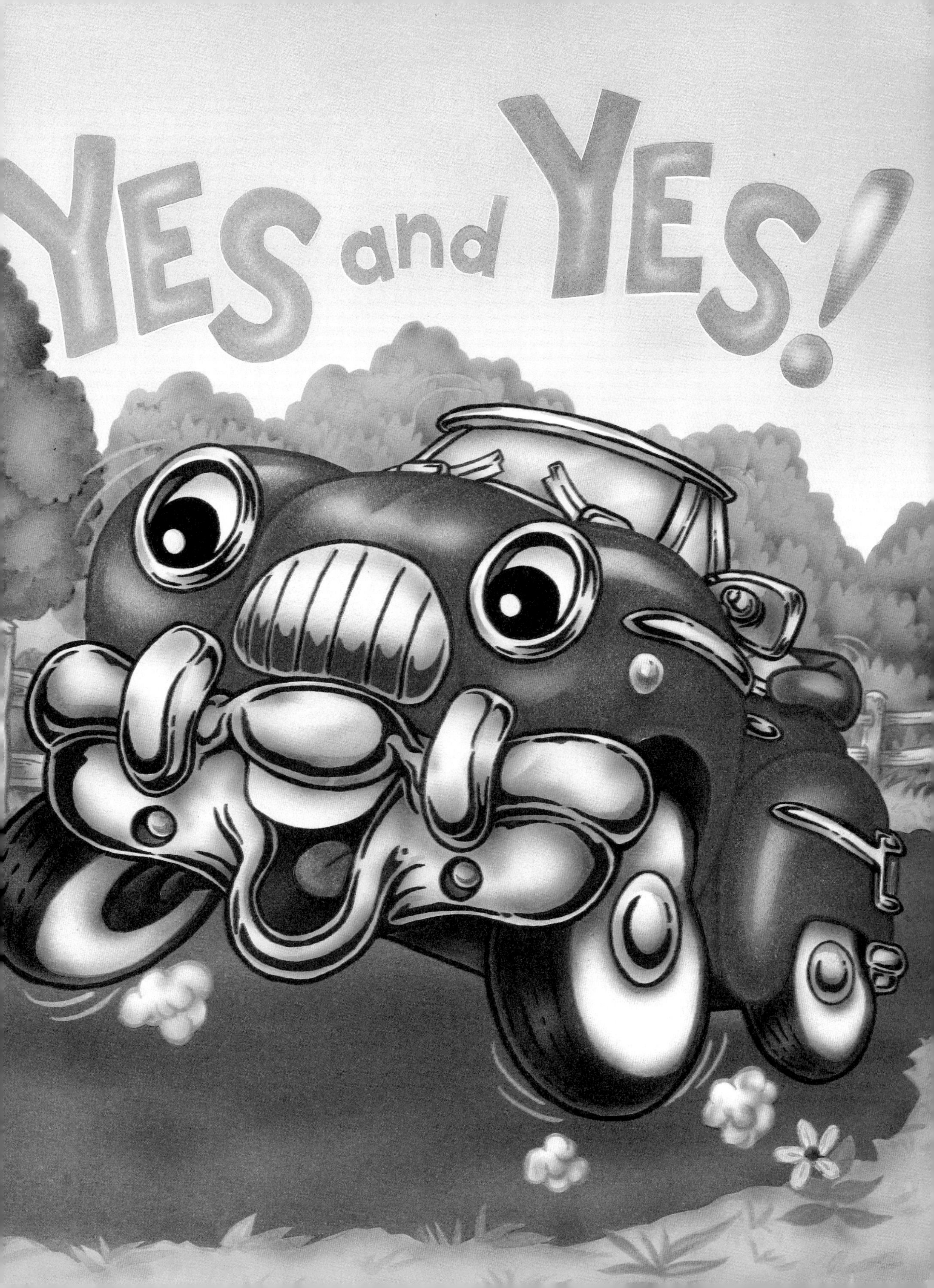
YES and YES!

"Certainly," said Charlie.

After filling up his tank, they started on their way.

Orson followed for a while,
but stopped again. Now he
had a flat tire.

He called to Harriet and Charlie.

Charlie and Harriet came to the rescue and gave him a spare tire.

Orson was happy.

"May we drive together now?"

"Sure," said Charlie. "You may
be bright and shiny and big,
but under your hood I
guess you're just like us."

I wonder if people
are the same way.

To children everywhere… all colors, shapes, and sizes. — M.D.

Written by:

Erin Barber
Kathryn Beeler
Emily Betts
Eric Betzwieser
Lauren Bussey
Gavin Carpenter
Duncan Clancy
Eric Courcelle
Matthew Courcelle
Leigh Ann Duffey
Robert Franchini
Jimmy Furlong
Michael Gambacorta
Jennifer Hart

Maureen Kilmade
Phil Maiello
Gina Malone
Matthew Martin
Harry Minehan
Julie Reilly
Leanne Ricchiutti
Mark Riley
Beth-Marie Russ
Vicky Schilling
Amy Sciocchetti
Melanie Sinnott
Juliet Tarantino
Katlyn Touhey

Margaret Doellefeld, Teacher

About This Book...

Writing this book with my children for the "Scholastic We Are All Alike... We Are All Different" awards program was one of the most challenging and rewarding times of my teaching career. The children learned a great deal about themselves, about others, and about books. We talked, we drew, we wrote, we read, and all of our labors, while serious, were filled with the innocent, lighthearted look at life enjoyed by five-year-olds.

Initially, the children's interest was captured by playing the song, "It Isn't Easy Being Green," followed by a series of group discussions on whether having a different skin color makes people different inside.

Next, we read several books that had to do with people of different backgrounds. From these books, we continued to find that people of various racial and ethnic groups might have different-colored skin and may have lived somewhere else before coming to America. We learned about Irish-Americans, Italian-Americans, Polish-Americans, African-Americans, as well as many others.

Then, to further our awareness of similarities and differences, we began exploring the animal kingdom. The children quickly concluded that all dogs look different but are still dogs. Our class gerbils were black and white, but both were gerbils. It was one short leap to looking at inanimate objects, and the class was bursting with ideas. Refrigerators and televisions could be different yet still be refrigerators and televisions. We had different makes of cars, but all operated pretty much the same way. Thus, "Orson" came into being, and the children gave him life. The point about external differences and internal similarities had been made, and that was the start of the book.

The text for *What's Under Your Hood, Orson?* was created from class discussions. Time was spent each day with children discussing, creating, and selecting illustrations for the book. When completed, we proudly addressed an envelope and, as a group, mailed off our work. Inspired by our class drawings, a professional illustrator hired by Scholastic then created the illustrations for the book.

This project proved to be beneficial in so many ways. We not only gained understanding about human likenesses and differences, but also learned a great deal about the publishing process. This group of five-year-olds also learned how to work together toward a common goal and stick with a long-term project. In the end, it is hoped that creating this book is one kindergarten class's contribution to making this a kinder world.

Margaret Doellefeld, Kindergarten Teacher
Holy Cross School, Albany, New York